Misty Maris

1907 NE 91 Ave.

Vancouver Wa.

98662

256-7060

1970 12

Weekly Reader Children's Book Club presents

EMILY'S BUNCH

By Laura Joffe Numeroff and
Alice Numeroff Richter

Illustrated by Laura Joffe Numeroff

MACMILLAN PUBLISHING CO., INC.
New York

This book is a presentation of
Weekly Reader Children's Book Club.

Weekly Reader Children's Book Club
offers book clubs for children from
preschool through junior high school.
All quality hardcover books are selected by
a distinguished Weekly Reader Selection Board.

For further information write to:
Weekly Reader Children's Book Club
1250 Fairwood Ave.
Columbus, Ohio 43216

Macmillan Publishing Co., Inc.
866 Third Avenue, New York, N.Y. 10022
Collier Macmillan Canada, Ltd.

Printed in the United States of America

LIBRARY OF CONGRESS CATALOGING IN PUBLICATION DATA

Numeroff, Laura Joffe.
Emily's bunch.

SUMMARY: Emily tries to come up with an
"original" idea for a party costume.

[1. Halloween—Fiction] I. Richter, Alice
Numeroff, joint author. II. Title.

PZ7.N964Em [E] 78-2637 ISBN 0-02-768430-X

To my bunch—Jerry, Douglas and Nancy

—A. N. R.

For my grandmother and Pat Griffin

—L. J. N.

Jeffrey decided to go to Herbie Beanstock's costume party dressed as Herbie Beanstock. Jeffrey thought it was a most original idea.

Herbie thought it stunk.

Jeffrey's little sister, Emily,
decided to go as a ghost.
Emily thought it was a most original idea.

Jeffrey thought it stunk.

"Maybe if I wear my ghost costume to breakfast tomorrow," Emily thought, "Jeffrey will see what a really good costume it is."

And that's exactly what she did.
Emily stood next to Jeffrey
in her ghost costume the next morning.

"Wait till he sees me," Emily thought.

Nothing happened.

Emily flapped her arms and said, "Boo."
Jeffrey continued eating his cereal.

She said, “Boo,” again. Jeffrey got up and put his empty bowl into the sink.

"You're s'posed to be scared," Emily said.
"Who would be scared of a little kid

walking around in a pillow case?"
asked Jeffrey.

"I would," Emily said.

"Besides," said Jeffrey, "I happen to know

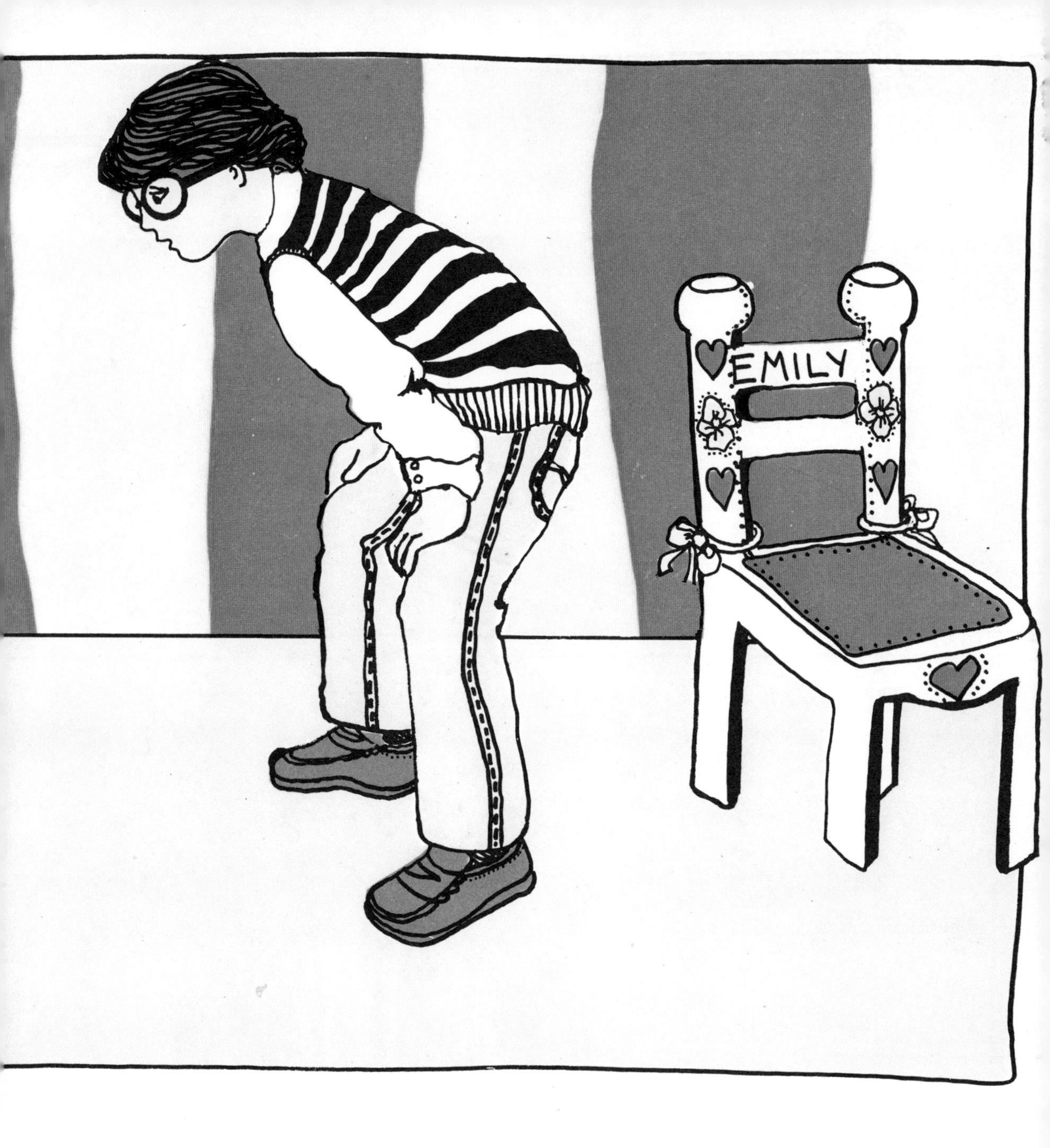

that Amy Bailey is going as a ghost.
And so is Neil Sanderson."

"Then I'll be a witch," said Emily.

"Well, I just happen to know that little Jerry Munzer is going to be a witch," said Jeffrey.

“Then I’ll be a monster,” said Emily.

"Well, I happen to know that Patricia Griffin and Jonathan Levy are going as monsters," said Jeffrey.

"Then what else can I be?" asked Emily.
"Nothing," replied Jeffrey.

Emily thought for a minute.
"Then I'll be a bunch of grapes.
Nobody else is going as a bunch of grapes."

"How are you going to be a bunch
of grapes?" asked Jeffrey.

"You'll see," Emily said.

Each day after school, Emily sat
on her bed and wondered how
she was going to be a bunch of grapes.

She just couldn't figure out anything.

"Oh, fiddlesticks," she thought, "I'll bet Jeffrey has his Herbie Beanstock costume already."

OCT.

Bear

On Friday night, before the party, Jeffrey peeked into Emily's room.

"I knew it," he said. "I just knew it. You're not a bunch of grapes. And for your information, wearing a brown paper bag that you painted purple does not make you a bunch of grapes."

"Oh, yes, it does," said Emily.

"Oh, no, it doesn't," Jeffrey said.

"Oh, yes, it does," said Emily's friends
Janet, Eileen and Barbara,
coming from behind the dresser.

"Oh, yes, it does,"
said Emily's friends
Carol and Meredith,
coming from behind the bookcase.

"Wearing a brown paper bag that you painted purple DOES make you a bunch of grapes," Emily said, "when you have other grapes in your bunch!"